Legal

ISBN: 13: 978-1-7321877-5-7

Table of Contents

Introduction

I recently uncovered the prototype for *Mutant Commandos™*. Secondary school was the timeframe and the year was 1987. I was in the 8th grade. This comic book was broken into two categories: (1) the Mutant Commandos™; and (2) the Humanoid Team™. Having always been into trademarks and copyright related issues growing up in a media and publishing family, these concepts were integrated into this series. This is directly reflected in the character development regarding in these action figures. Make sure not to miss Fungi™ on the original publication's page 7.

I was constantly trying entrepreneurial things, selling my mother's beads on safety pins to attach to shoelaces. The product was a huge hit in the 4th grade. People would give me their lunch money or change in exchange for the product and soon everyone was wearing them.

Much later I became an adamant brew master and held private instruction on how to bottle and brew beer, including managing to overcome a few mishaps along the way, which involved a fermentation explosion at 4:00 a.m. for a malt beer that covered the lanai porch ceiling.

These showcase events were also very popular with 50 to 70 people showing up. Naturally, they involved a very complicated process from start to finish (sanitizing, cooking, brewing and bottling).

Bringing back the characters in *Mutant Commandos* in a comic book series is eminent. This is the second series in addition to *The Book About The Crystal World*.

Finally I will be releasing my first *fiction* novel, based on covert operations and the underworld.

Without further adieu, here is the second time-capsule release.

Original Table of Contents

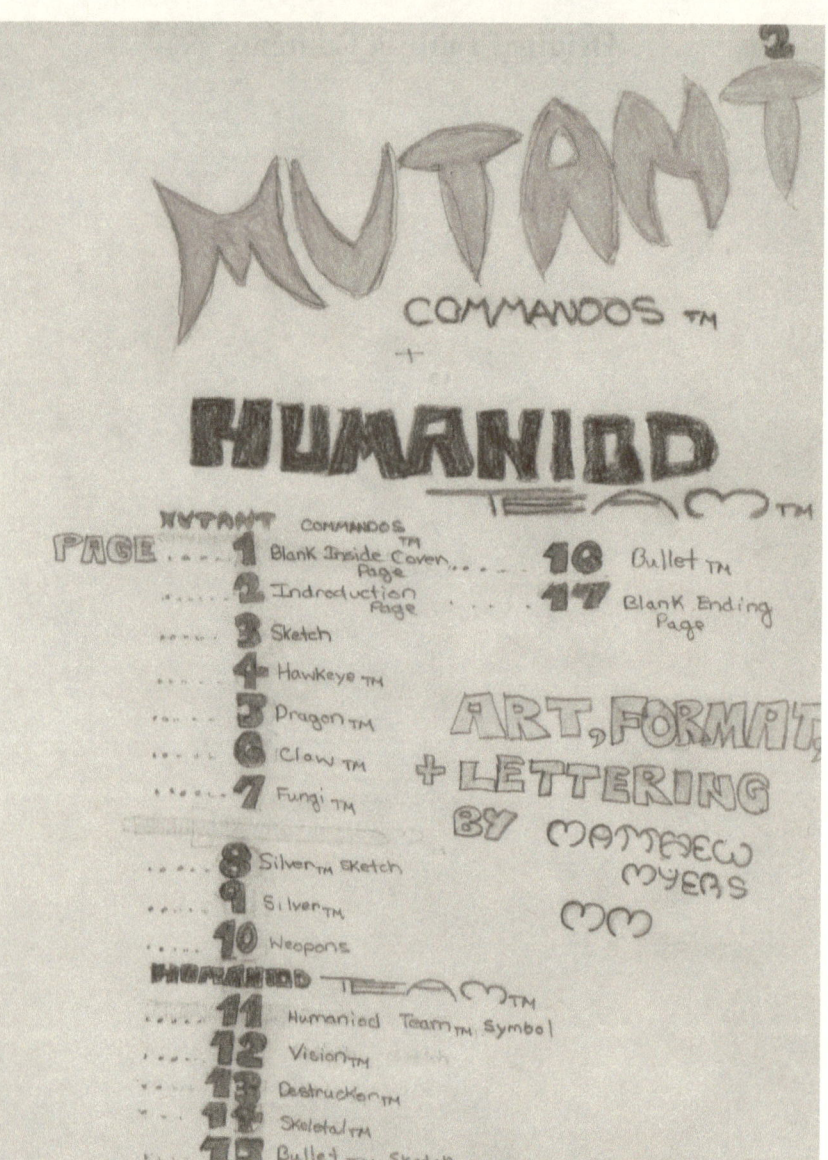

MUTANT²

COMMANDOS ™

+

HUMANIOD

TEAM™

ART, FORMAT, + LETTERING BY MATTHEW MYERS

MM

Introducing the Mutant Commandos

HAWKEYE™

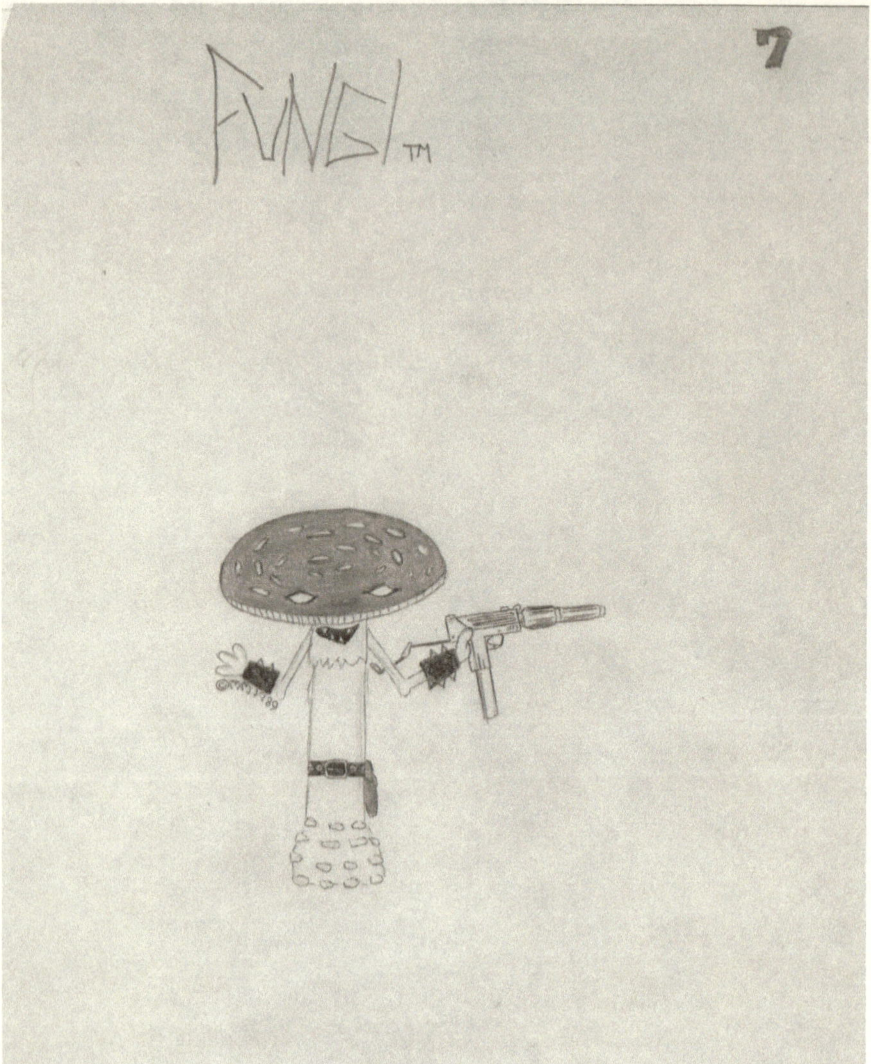
FUNGI™
7

Vehicles

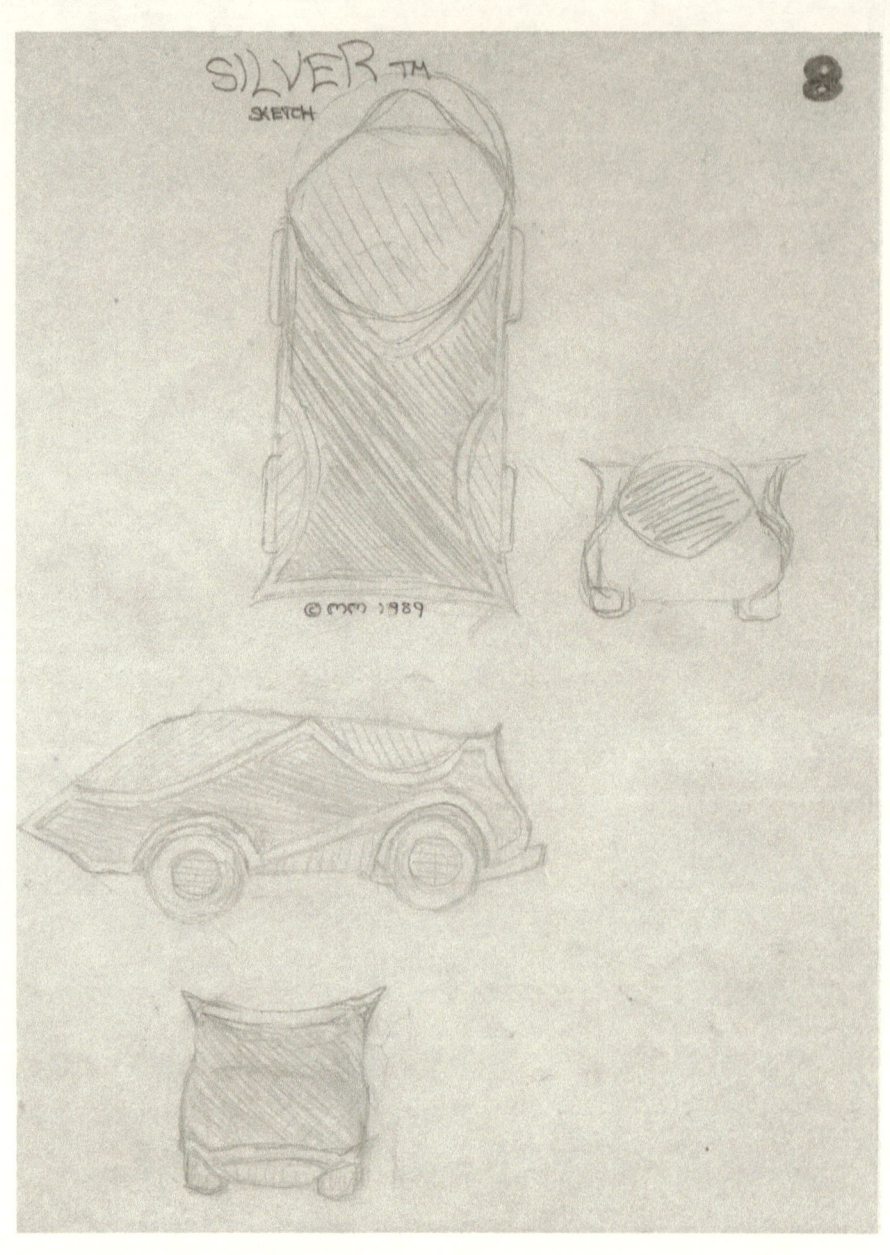

SILVER ™
SKETCH

© mm 1989

SILVER™

Not Drawn By Scale

©mm 1989

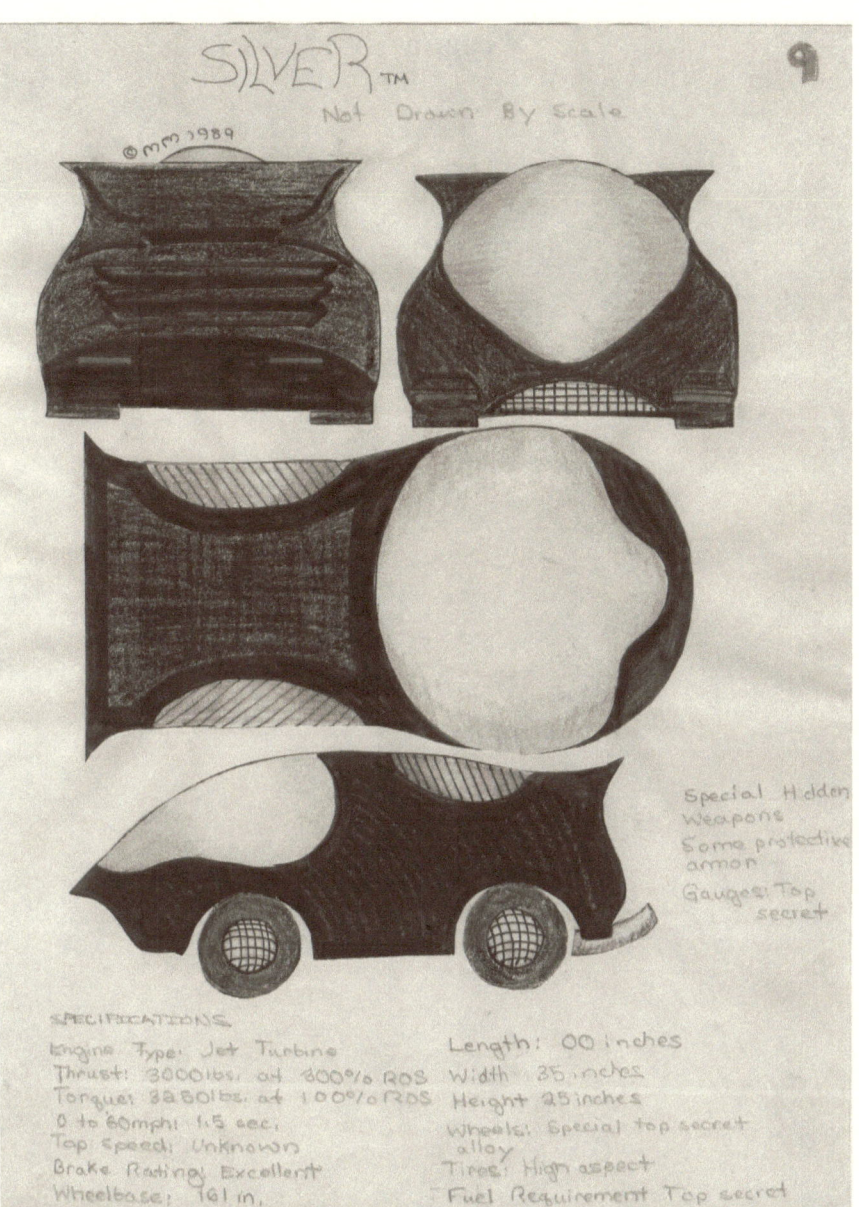

Special Hidden
Weapons
Some protective
armor

Gauges: Top
secret

SPECIFICATIONS

Engine Type: Jet Turbine
Thrust: 3000lbs. at 300% ROS
Torque: 3280lbs. at 100% ROS
0 to 60mph: 1.5 sec.
Top speed: Unknown
Brake Rating: Excellent
Wheelbase: 161 in.

Length: 00 inches
Width: 35 inches
Height: 25 inches
Wheels: Special top secret
alloy
Tires: High aspect
Fuel Requirement: Top secret

Weapons

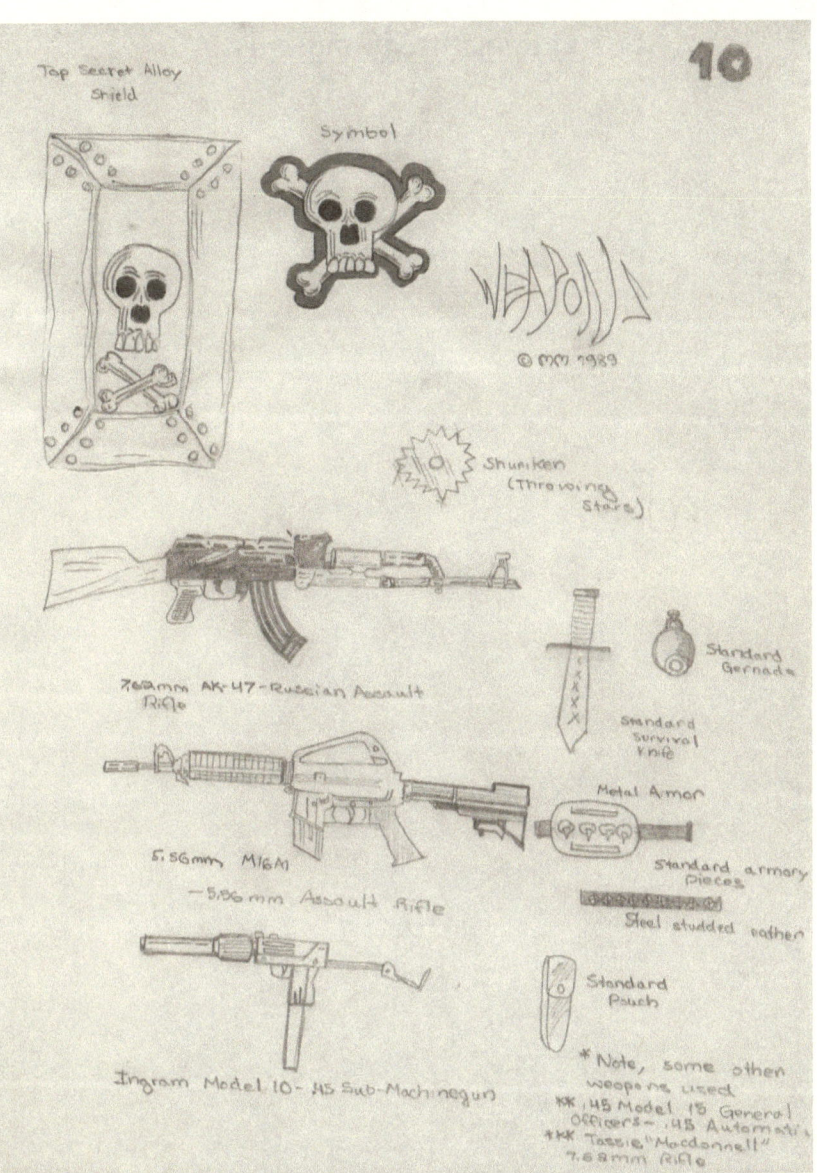

Introducing the Humanoids

VISION™

DESTRUCKOR™

Vehicles

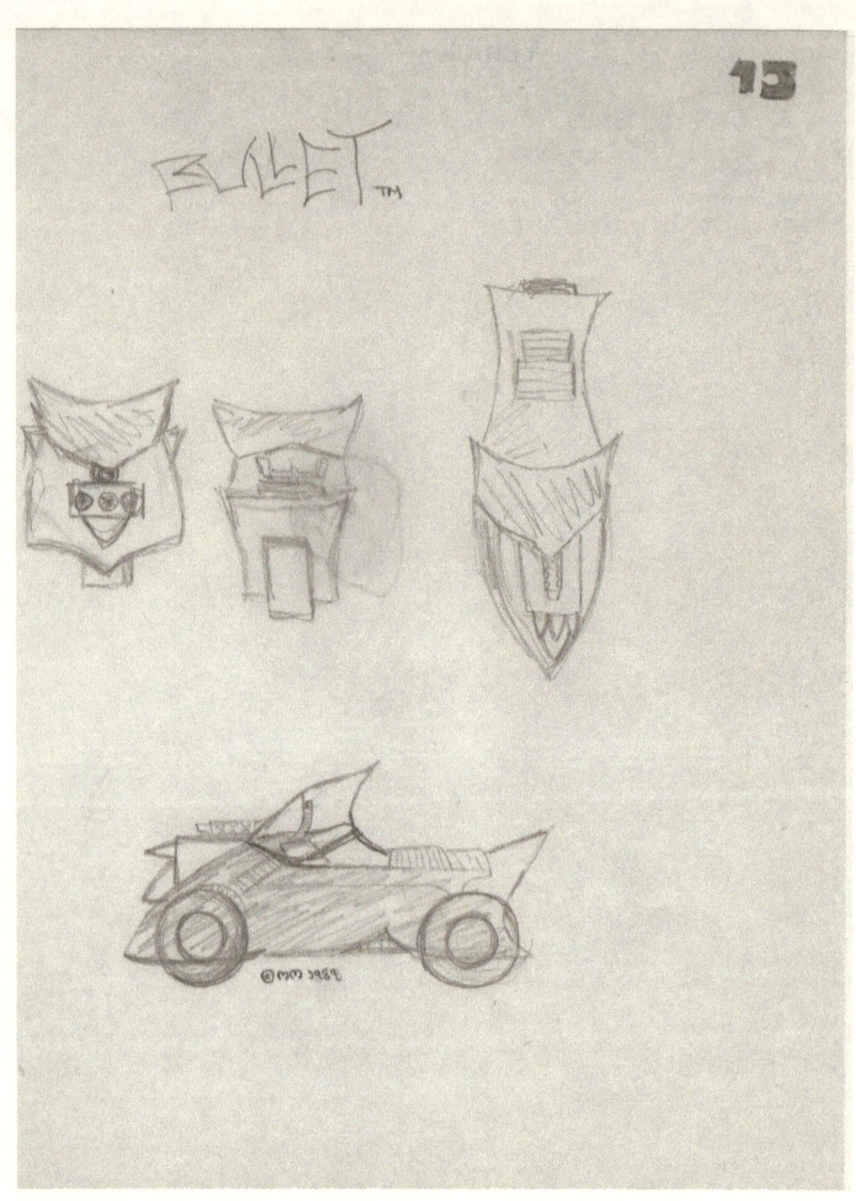

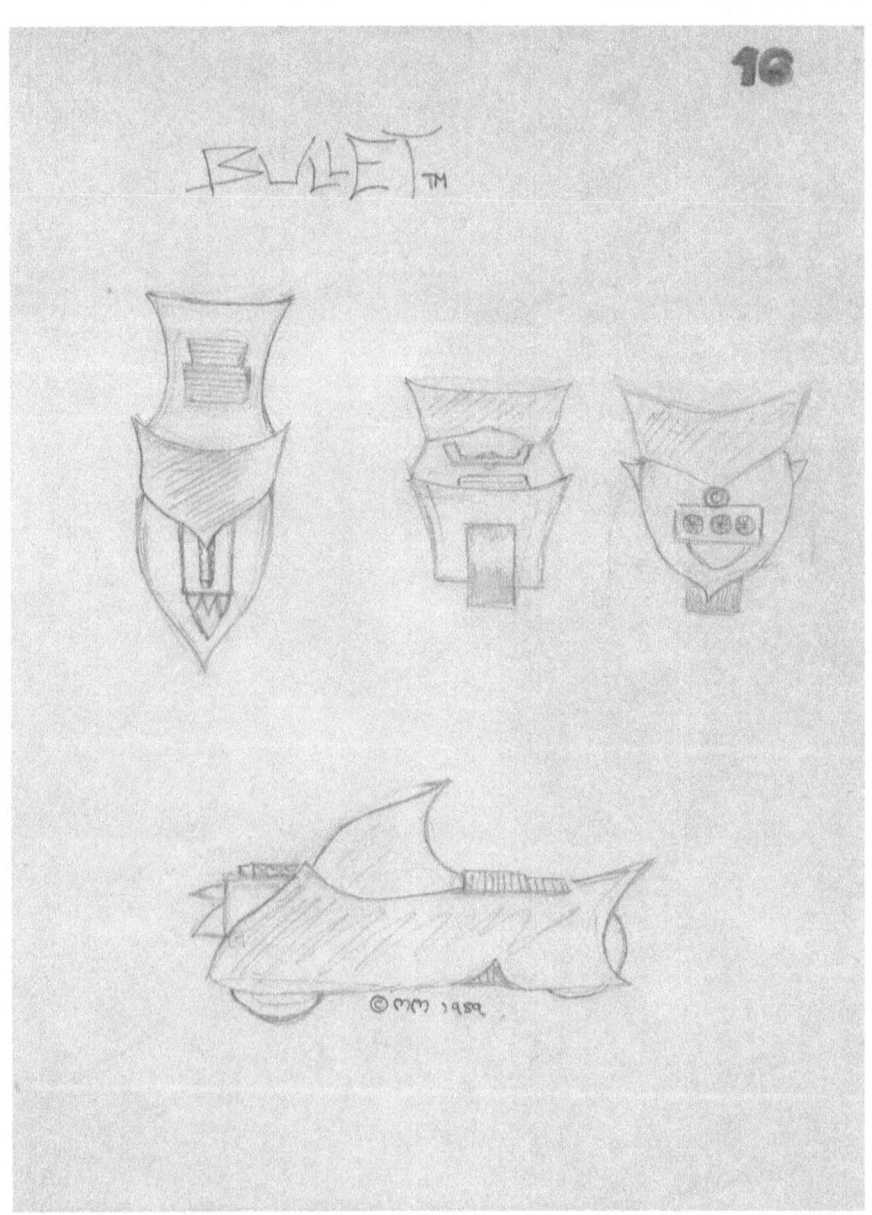

Bonus

Unspecified. Unsealed.

Surfer warrior.

www.ingramcontent.com/pod-product-compliance
Lightning Source LLC
Chambersburg PA
CBHW020920180626
46816CB00007BA/2495